THE HEREAFTER

BY

JOHN PAUL
Minister and writer; author of "Silver Keys" etc. Professor in Meridian Colleges, Meridian, Miss.

COPYRIGHTED, 1910.

PENTECOSTAL PUBLISHING COMPANY,
LOUISVILLE, KY.

TABLE OF CHAPTERS.

	PAGE
I. Man	5
II. The Soul	8
III. The Immortal Body	12
IV. The Dropped Stitch	17
V. The Broken Bridge	20
VI. God's Nurseries	26
VII. The Open Switch	29
VIII. The Stay of Execution	34
IX. The Intermediate State	39
X. The Millennium	43
XI. The General Resurrection	53
XII. The Judgment	58
XIII. Hell	63
XIV. Future Rewards	74
XV. Recognition in Heaven	80
XVI. The Unbridged Gulf	84
XVII. The Ultimate Kingdom	88
XVIII. The City of The-Lord-Is-There	92

CHAPTER I.

MAN.

It is a great mistake to attach little importance to man. He is not a "worm of the dust," but a miniature of God. Nor is it true that in the fall man lost God's image. He lost an important part of this image, we admit, but very little of that part of the divine image which is peculiar to himself. He lost holiness—a general quality in the divine image which belonged to every created intelligence. But no doubt that in the spiritual and mental make-up of man there are many peculiar things, beyond our analysis, which are like God. These things have to do with man's yet unfathomed capacity for dominion, for power, and for service. Man's varied capacities are now broken, depleted, and obscured by the fall and its results; but they are in him—God sees them—no matter who he is, nor what his thralldom; no matter if at present he may be only "the man with a hoe," or even the man behind the bars or within the asylum for the insane. In other words, he may be never so broken, morally, mentally, or physically, yet he is man; and down beneath the rubbish, God sees His own image, loves him the more for that reason, and enjoins upon every intelligent creature the duty of having reverence for man and seeking after his welfare. We have never seen man. In his present fallen estate God alone can see him, for his divine attributes are only in embryo, and they are covered up by a thousand accumulated failures and faults. He must have been a glorious creature before he fell; he will certainly be a glorious creature when he appears again in the last day, full clad, in the image and likeness of God.

An elevated conception of man is what the world needs; and a tendency to this high estimate of human beings, little known among the heathen, is seen in the wake of civilization, especially that civilization which has for its mainspring the kingdom of Christ. This exalted conception leaves its mark in literature, in institutions for the development of mind and body, for the care of unfortunates, and even in institutions for the detention of criminals. It influences the architecture of enlightened lands; it affects their laws; it is traceable even in the places where the dead are buried.

If there is any class of teachers on the face of the earth who deserve no toleration whatever, it is those who in the name of religion or philosophy attempt to sink people into the notion that man is not an immortal being. If they had universal success with their doctrine, in less than two centuries its depressing effect would be evident in every institution of society, and in every handiwork of man.

Man is a soul. That he has a body or is a body is a fact, but a subjective fact. The Scriptures throughout assume this, just as they assume the existence of God. In the story of creation it is said, not that man became a mortal body, but that he became a living (an immortal) soul. This conception has continued from that day, excepting when it was beclouded by debased moral conditions. Paul the Apostle received the truth from the fountain head; and he lived in a state of conscious immortality, knowing that to be absent from the body was to be present with the Lord, looking upon man as a spiritual being separable from his mortal tenement. Indeed, as to the character of man's existence, he ranked him with the immortal, spiritual, angels—only "a little lower." And so the Apostle Peter, commissioned of Christ to break spiritual bread and minister to the needs of the immortal part of man, thought of his own body as a temporary house, but treated *himself* as an immortal being, soon to lift anchor for another shore when he said, "Shortly I must put off this my tabernacle."

CHAPTER II.

THE SOUL.

There is in every specimen of physical life a mysterious immaterial something, permeating every part of the organism, and called the life of the thing. It is, in the accommodated sense, sometimes called a soul, hence the expression, *souls of animals*. This something has its affinities, its proclivities, its instincts. This something has its mysteries, which man cannot fathom. But that it belongs to the mysterious system of merely physical forces is evident from the fact that it wanes when disorder appears in the body, gradually failing as the machinery of the body gives down, diminishing oftentimes to a mere spark, and passing away like the blaze of an exhausted candle.

In a lower scale, this life is found in the realms of chemistry. Minerals have their affinities and their incompatibles, just as animals have their likes and dislikes. The traceable relationship between animal life and other forms of physical life, down to the life of a stone or an atom, proves to us that animal life is simply one of the higher expressions or headings of that force which slumbers in the bosom of the physical universe—a fire that burns when it has a wick and oil to support it, but which goes out and is dissolved in the bosom of latent force when its nucleus is destroyed.

But when we come to a study of man, we soon discover that physical life, with its primitive and simple likes and dislikes, is not all there is of him. What the horse knew in the days of Solomon, he knows today; no more, no less. But man has a mind capable of receiving the accumulated knowledge of centuries. He can learn a fact or a lesson, and then, without reviewing it, after every atom of his brain is changed, which is the case every seven years, more or less, he can repeat that lesson. It has become a part of his soul; and though his physical tastes may change as his body puts on new material, what becomes a part of his mind or soul abides, showing that while in man's make-up there is an ever-changing part, there is also in his make-up a never changing (God-like) part. Then man has a chain of heart-affections and other, kindred spiritual qualities which do not appear in animals, and which, so far as we have ever been able to follow them in our observation are immortal. Man has his physical likes and dislikes; he likes and dislikes with his body, just as do the lower animals; and as his body weakens toward death, these propensities are known to wane, giving evidence that they will perish with the body. But man's heart-loves and heart-aspirations often appear in their noonday glory when his pulse is weak and the last light of physical life is about to fade from his eye.

It is known to all students of the human soul that below man's conscious mind, back of the things he knows he knows, there is a sub-conscious mind, containing, not only the memories and lessons which he verily knows but does not know that he knows, but a mind which has capacities and powers vastly beyond anything we can imagine, powers which have not in this world a field for operation—a mind too great for present pursuits, which prints a feeble proof of itself upon the tissues of the brain.

A further study of this marvelous latent mind has proven that when it does come to where it can operate, when by a divine touch it is set free, it will matter but little whether or not it has a body through which to operate. There is no indication that it cannot operate through a perfect body, but there is clear evidence that it can operate apart from and independent of a body. *Excarnate man* is a foolish expression to the materialistic philosopher, but it does not take long for the Christian observer to see the reasonableness of the thing. When our nerves are relaxed and with our brains are wrapped in slumber, our trips to dreamland furnish suggestions of the possibilities of the soul operating apart from the body. The visions and trances into which some have entered, have brought to light the existence of a mind which can operate when the bodily powers are dormant. Indeed our physical life, including a shallow mental life, at once serves as a transparent connecting medium between immortal man and the temporal world, and an opaque curtain between immortal man and the eternal world.

Man's God-likeness is not in his body, *formed* of (something already made or created) the dust of the ground, but in his soul, created or made, not of substances or things in existence, but in the image of God. Since the birth of Christ it has been understood that God, though a Spirit, may dwell in and operate through a body. The *excarnate* or *incarnate God* are intelligent expressions. While we do not presume that man was made like unto God in the *extent* of his existence, yet we do hold that man is like God in the mode and quality of his existence. Being in the image of God, man is therefore capable of dwelling in a body or out of a body.

CHAPTER III.

THE IMMORTAL BODY.

If the title of this chapter had been *the resurrection body*, it would not have covered all cases, for there are many to be changed in the last day of this age, from mortal to immortal, without dying. Then, there have been resurrection bodies that were not immortal. If our title had been *glorification*, it would have been too broad, since in a considerable degree, redeemed souls in heaven are now glorified, though their bodies still sleep in the dust. Again, this title would have been too narrow; for the risen Lord was not glorified till the end of the forty days He was upon earth. Glorification means to be exalted to heavenly blessedness, to be given a reception to the kingdom above, to be acknowledged because of achievements.

An immortal body is something supernatural. It cannot be, according to the laws analyzed and defined by finite men. The scientist cannot speak for anything beyond the solar system, but he has discovered that even the sun is decreasing in diameter at the rate of about two hundred feet per year, and that it will not have heat enough to sustain any form of life on the

The Hereafter. 13

earth for more than ten million years. There is a law on earth whereby every machine must wear out. Indeed there are several laws, such as friction, decay and chemical disintegration; so that if one fails, another will infallibly do the work. Fate has it that everything which we are now allowed to touch must vanish. This is such a universal fact, that the thought of a body that never grows old or a city that shall abide forever, strikes the dweller on this planet as rather a strange notion. But is it not true that this world and its surroundings are fashioned to match its temporary inhabitants, to solemnize their hearts by reminding them that they are only sojourners, and to contribute to their longing for a home beyond the skies? Do you think that to make a perishable system is the best God can do? Far from it. Who knows but that we are in sight of *immortal* worlds! The mariner cannot depend upon anything within the solar system as an infallible timepiece and guide. He looks away across twenty trillions of miles of space and locates himself and sets his watch by a fixed star. I will not be dogmatic about the fixed stars (for some think they move a little, though it may be merely a yet undiscovered motion of our own system), but I steadfastly believe that the majority of organisms and structures in this vast universe know nothing of the laws of decay, and never grow old.

We have some opportunity to study an immortal human body. Jesus Christ, whose mission it was to "show us the Father," and give us glimpses of more than one fact connected with God's ways and thoughts, lived upon earth forty days in an immortal body; just such, we are told, as we shall have, when He comes and the trumpet sounds. He proved during that time to belong to a country whose *natural* laws have little if anything in common with the laws which govern us. His body was not obstructed by our obstructions, was not dependent upon, though capable of, our diets, evidently was not exposed to our maladies and pains, and was not affected by our law of gravitation. Were these things true because He was God? That might be, in part. But since we are to be like Him in the quality of our immortal bodies, it stands to reason that we shall pass into a system whose laws will surround us very much as they do Him.

A body that cannot be sick! A body that never grows old! How inviting such an estate to a tired traveler upon the earth! Our aches and pains sometimes make us long for a change. Elijah, notwithstanding his piety, was so subdued by hunger and fatigue that he wished for death. But the high aim of our beneficent Creator and Redeemer is to bring us to a condition where danger will be a stranger, and where we will be immune, not only from contagions which we have already had, and which destroyed in our system every element which made their return possible, but from all sickness and disease. If smallpox or any other disease can hedge its own way in a human body, and make its own return impossible, how much more can God, when He transforms us and puts upon us the robes of glory, destroy the possibility of sickness. If it is impossible for certain animals to have human diseases, how much more will it be impossible for man himself to have a disease when he arises to his perfected state? That matter is from henceforth eternal is quite a thinkable proposition. If God can make this possible concerning matter in its inorganic state, may He not make it possible in its highest organized form? If He should, that would settle the question of an immortal body —a never failing wick for the fire of life to burn in. The most ordinary kerosene lamp would burn forever, if it never corroded or decayed, if its wick never failed and its oil supply were permanent, and nothing were allowed to extinguish it. So far as its blaze is concerned, it is immortal. To the gray haired man with stooping form, we say, cheer up; that youthful soul of yours will tent some day in a tabernacle which shall never be folded, which can never become weather-beaten. The wheels of life turn slowly now, but in a short while you shall keep step with the immortals. The blood that replenishes your tired brain is sluggish, and your rich store of knowledge is at times quite forgotten; but it is not gone forever. Tomorrow you shall put on immortality, your forgotten knowledge, which is still in your now impeded soul, will be recovered with interest, and your mind will be as fresh as the sparkling waters in the river from which you will drink. The fountain of health has almost failed you; if a healing potion equal to your pains now grows in any herb upon the earth, no friend has found it for you; but in one day, in one moment, in the twinkling of an eye, this mortal shall put on immortality, and a traveler, once lame and faltering, shall walk amid the everbearing trees whose leaves are the emblems of health, to experience pain and sickness no more forever.

CHAPTER IV.

THE DROPPED STITCH.

Who can imagine the greatness of God! He occupies immensity—endless space. That means that His dominion has no bound. You might multiply the billions of miles by the billions of miles for a billion of years, if there is an archangel who can work the sum, and yet you would not be started toward completing the extent of God's dominion. His existence is from eternity to eternity. With Him there was no such a thing as what we call a beginning, nor will there be an end. This God of whom we speak is a person—the personality who gave all other persons their being. He thinks, for He made the mind; He sees, for He formed the eye; He hears, for He planted the ear. All creation bears the marks of His wisdom. The stars are more accurate than clocks; the planets and satellites are more reliable in their schedules than a metropolitan railroad train. The evidence is that God lives for His created universe, and that His created universe, in all its forms and phases, exists for His glory. He loves the oceans that roll and foam in majesty; He loves the mountains, with their abounding scenery; He loves the flowers, which He has endowed with fragrance and beauty; He loves the forests, which are parks of His own design; in the birds of the air, the beasts of the field, and the fishes of the waters, God takes pleasure. Above all these, it is true—He says it is true—He loves man.

God made one part of the universe for the other, and created in all a relationship to every part. The stars were made, as were the sun and moon, with reference to the earth; and no doubt it is understood upon the planets (if the planets are inhabited) that the earth was made with reference to the stars.

And now we come to "the dropped stitch." We know of at least one (probably the only) stitch that has been dropped in the plan of God. We use this figure with reverence. When we speak of the dropping of a stitch in His plans, we mean the occurrence of something in the universe contrary to His will; we therefore mean the fall of man and its results, and the fall of the angels, so far as we are acquainted with their fall. Why a thing could happen in the universe contrary to God's will we do not attempt to explain, but it has happened; and the disorder will abide till the dropped stitch is recovered.

We call these few thousands of years of

man's fallen estate a dropped stitch, not because it is a light thing, but because it is destined to be a brief period, compared to the two eternities. God will recover the world from its lapse, and things will glide on in sweet harmony forever, all the refuse—the incorrigible—being relegated to the far off realms of outer darkness.

If this age of wickedness is brought to a close, there must be One to accomplish the work. That One must have a plan of redemption, and in this plan provision must be made to pardon and sanctify the souls of men. And truly there is one, of the "seed of Abraham," whose death has satisfied the demands of justice, providing mercy and salvation for every penitent soul. The restoration of order in the fallen world must begin somewhere; consequently God's design is that it should begin in the hearts of His people. By His full salvation He restores unto man's heart the order that prevails in heaven and that is destined to prevail upon earth, when His knowledge shall cover the earth as waters cover the sea. It is His pleasure that there should not remain in us a rival to His will, but that in us should be the beginning of the recovery of the dropped stitch.

CHAPTER V.

THE BROKEN BRIDGE.

We cannot well study man's future without studying man. We cannot well study man, without taking into account his divine origin and his fall. When God first made man, He placed him in a beautiful garden, surrounded by a world free from all manner of curses—free from bad plants, from bad animals, and from bad weather. While only a spot of the world was a garden, all of its dry land was capable of becoming a garden as an increase in Adam's family created a demand for more room; and the seas, gentle and kind, were to furnish vast areas for the progress of human industry, existing doubtless under a divine regulation which made it impossible for them to have been treacherous in the least.

Earth was man's home. I cannot say that it was to have been man's home forever, I doubt this. I rather think it was God's great nursery; or, to be more expressive, a ship yard on the border of eternity's sea, where intelligent vessels, requisite in some far greater realm were to be formed, trained, and tested, to be translated across the sea. There could have been

The Hereafter. 21

no death until sin came, but doubtless God's way of translating Enoch and Elijah gives us a glimpse of what should have been the regular custom of the world, had man stood the probationary test and maintained an unfallen condition in the world.

We have been allowed enough insight to the economy of God in general to make us about sure that probationary testing has always been His rule, upon creating a responsible moral intelligence; and it is quite probable that most of His creatures stood the test, were rewarded accordingly, and are now among the brighter lights around the throne. But many of the angels "kept not their first estate."

The intelligent reader of these chapters will readily read between, if not in the lines, our admission when we fill in with matters of supposition, and discriminate between these and the facts about man and his past and future which may be certainly proven. It is not our purpose to depart from established orthodoxy anywhere, where orthodoxy has spoken, and we desire it understood that every essential or important statement of this book is made advisedly, and may be established by the word of God and the various branches of accredited knowledge.

We come to the fact that man was and is a probationer. The thought of it is clothed in mystery; but the fact of it is as clear as a sunbeam. We need not say that it was necessary for God to make all His wonderful creatures and try them through a probationary period, but we must say that He had a right to do so, and it appears that He did it. While we do not know the reason why the all-wise and all-powerful God should make a creature morally breakable—and for that reason we should bate our breath and abstain from foolish and critical questions—we do know that intuitive and experimental wisdom teaches man when he makes something which has to be entrusted with great responsibilities, first to test before he trusts that thing.

Often when a great railroad bridge is completed, train after train of heavy but inferior freight is rushed over it, with increasing weight and speed, till the bridge is thoroughly tested and it is decided that in the years to come they can trust it in all days, in all seasons, and upon dark and stormy nights, to bear up safely the cargoes of valuable freight and precious human lives. When an ocean steamer is completed, they test it, to see if it is seaworthy. If any of these great products of human skill should fail to stand the test it must be at the outset; and if they fail, the next work is that of reconstruction.

When man was placed in the garden of Eden, divine wisdom suffered a reasonable amount of strain to be placed upon his moral nature. The scheme of testing was first to put a tree of prohibited fruit in the midst of the garden where man was otherwise unlimited in his liberties. Following this was the heavier test of allowing the tempter to approach and engross man with fascinating arguments. Under all this man broke down. It was whispered in heaven that the joy of angels and the lovely offspring of God had fallen under his probationary test; and where there had once been a scheme of construction or creation, there was now a scheme of reconstruction or recreation.

The thought of all heaven was to restore man. It laid itself out in that direction. With that in view the angels of God visited the earth; with that in view the Son of God agreed to die. The bridge had broken down, and must be rebuilded; the ship had proven unseaworthy, and must be raised and reconstructed.

When reconstructed, the test must again come. The regenerated and purified man must remain upon the earth, not merely to fight a good fight, but to keep the faith. It is not long after a man proves thoroughly seaworthy till he goes hence to where there is no more execration—no more going out from God. If in the meantime he breaks he must be made again; if he breaks to be remade no more (Heb. 6.), he is doomed to the debris-pile of the universe forever. It is only those who finally stand the final test that shall wear the crown or enjoy the climax of eternal life (Rev. 2:10).

There are three departments in the construction of man; the physical, the intellectual and the moral. The moral is the mainspring of the mental and the physical. When man broke down morally, he immediately proceeded to physical and mental dilapidation. When man is restored in his moral nature, it does not follow that he is restored in mind and body; but he immediately sets out on the way to complete restoration. In God's redemptive scheme, He did not begin with a restoration of man's body or mind, which would have been a waste of time, for man would not have retained his perfect physical and mental endowments; but with a restoration of man's heart or moral nature, upon which everything depends. Moreover, the Lord deliberately deferred the restoration of man's mental and physical natures till the close of the probationary period, using all these innocent deficiencies as agencies through which the restored moral nature might be tested. It is God's plan that today we should be perfect in our hearts, and tomorrow, when we stand in his presence, we should be perfect in our minds and bodies. No need that we should be perfect in these departments sooner, for they are not breakable if endowed with an unbreakable moral nature. The mind and body need no testing; the heart is the responsible agent. Hence man's eternal destiny hinges not upon the condition of his mind or body, but upon the condition of his heart. The trifling provocations and inferior conditions which beset us here constitute the inferior matter with which the trains are loaded to test the bridge and prove it efficient for coming years, when the weight of worthless matter shall fall upon it no more.

CHAPTER VI.

GOD'S NURSERIES.

From what we can gather by our glimpses into the economy of God, His way of populating the universe with immortal creatures is analogous to the nurseryman who decides to start for himself a thousand acre orchard. The nurseryman first gives the tiny trees their origin in a place far too small for their highest development; a place where they may show what they are, but in a very small measure. These little plants, at first no more noble in their appearance than the lower, groveling products of the vegetable kingdom, pass through a probationary period, at the end of which they are transplanted from the nursery into the garden of their lord where there is an absolute plenty of room for them to become all that it is in them to become. Thus the human soul, the beginning of one of God's greatest products, is in this life compassed about with many infirmities, and by surroundings which make impossible for it to do more than develop a good suggestion of its marvelous capacity. At first, the untrained observer is liable to confuse it with the "spirit of the beast that goeth downward"

(Eccl. 3:21), and suppose that man is but a higher form of earth's temporary creatures. But as he, passing out of infancy, enters his own element of faith and hope and love, traces of higher life begin to appear, until the one who intelligently studies him can soon see that this life is too small for him, and that it contains nothing sufficient to meet his higher aspirations.

Though small in its literal scope, and limited in its possibilities, this life is extremely important, for here we begin. A disease in the tree would have to be transplanted with the tree into the orchard. This disease would forever limit the possibilities of the tree and mar the beauty of the orchard. A disease uncured in the young plant will therefore carry it to the rubbish pile. If this is true of a plant, which is not to blame for its deficiencies, how much more is it true of a rational being, who has learned a way out of his limitations, who knows that at great expense his Lord has provided to *heal him in the nursery*, with a view to transferring him into the glories of the second Eden?

Man is capable of making a choice, and actively seeking the object of his choice. By repentance, consecration and faith, he may appropriate the holiness or health that comes from God; so, aside from being rejected at the end of his life in the nursery, he will be held to account for cleaving to his disease of sin and thwarting the object for which he was created.

"The earth which drinketh in the rain that cometh oft upon it, and bringeth forth herbs meet for them by whom it is dressed, receiveth blessing from God; but that which beareth thorns and briars is rejected, and is nigh unto cursing; whose end is to be burned. But, beloved, we are persuaded better things of you, and things that accompany salvation." Hebrews 6:7-9.

CHAPTER VII.

THE OPEN SWITCH.

That was a serious sin that Adam committed in Eden. The deed itself would not have seemed so shocking but the principle was far-reaching. There was a principle in it that set God at naught, declaring Him no longer King, and involving the wreck of His government. There was a malignant plant which would go on multiplying itself and menacing the garden of God forever; which, instead of shriveling in the course of centuries, would become more thrifty and noxious. Adam could not have reckoned the gravity of his sin from his view point. If he could have stood on our vantage ground, if he could have read a bulletin of the crime and suffering of yesterday, and had the degenerate millions of his offspring file before him, he could have better appreciated the sinfulness of sin. Unless outside help came there could be no end to the mischievous consequences of this one sin; it therefore follows that if the sinner had paid the penalty, there could be no end to the penalty. If the crime was endless in its consequence, the pit into which the criminal has to be dropped may be bottomless.

So much for Adam's first sin; but his second and later sins were no less sinful; and though these latter sins—if he continued in sin—were not necessary in order to the curse of coming generations and the multiplying calamities of the centuries, they were sufficient to produce these things, and were adjudged equally sinful with the first. And if Adam's later sins were sufficient to have produced unending calamities, and prgressive enough, if not counteracted, to leaven the universe, any of our sins are sufficient. We therefore stand on a footing of guilt with the first man that sinned.

Let us suppose a scene. It is a moonlit night, on the main line of a great railroad, a few miles from the terminal. A man looks at his watch and figures that within five minutes the fast train will go by, with a large number of passengers. He deliberately opens the switch that leads out upon a spur in the forest, stands back and waits to see the wreck. Now he hears the roar of the locomotive, now he sees the glare of the headlight, then the train, plunging through at fifty miles an hour, leaps out into the forest; a moment, and the wreck is complete. The engine, a burning mass, is crushed among the great oaks, the coaches, torn to splinters, pile one upon another in the flames, and the cry of a multitude of the helpless and dying is enough to hush the poetry of the moon and stars and hills. A fortunate circumstance leads to the immediate arrest of the criminal, he is tried and hurried away to the city, and instead of meeting their loved ones, the waiters at the station have to listen to the news of disaster and look upon the monster who in one moment found it easy to open the way for their destruction. Can you imagine the sentence they would have passed upon him in court? Indeed he was guilty of a capital crime. But let us suppose that he had failed in his diabolism; that when he opened the switch, a good man, being near, had rushed in and closed the switch at the peril of his life, just as the train was speeding by, and all had passed safely, unconscious of their narrow escape. Would our criminal have been less guilty? No doubt the finiteness of human courts would have prevented the severest penalty; but God, who reads the hearts of men had already booked his deed, seen its consequences, and named the penalty, without crediting the bad man with that deed of the good man which counteracted the results of his badness.

What credit is it to a sinner, if his sin does not bear fruit for centuries to come, making a track as wide as a planet? If it does not, it will be because good agencies will have closed the switch which he opened; but he will be none the less guilty. What credit is it to him, indeed, that he is not a larger sinner? Could he know more infallibly the difference between right and wrong if his physical strength were treble what it is, and he were double his present height? This would therefore make him no greater sinner. Since it is just as easy to suppose, let us suppose that he were as large as the American continent, and more than a match for all the angels in heaven. Let us suppose that his mighty frame towered among the stars, that he were master of the planets, and of all the physical forces; that he had no one to fear but God, and that his might and mastery made him a formidable rival to God Himself. We see at once that a sin of his—being an act of rebellion—would then be more disastrous in fact, but it could not be any more disastrous in principle. Though he is only five feet high, if he sin against God he goes his full length toward God's dethronement; and he is due no credit for being weak and small. His guilt can be as great, then, as if he were second in strength only to God Himself. That philosophy which objects to the doctrine of infinite perdition on the ground that it cannot consistently be the doom of a finite sinner forgets that a finite sinner does deeds of infinite consequence, and that the principle is measureless in its guilt, however small the sinner himself may be.

CHAPTER VIII.

THE STAY OF EXECUTION.

There is no mercy in nature. The laws of the natural world operate like some great engine whose master, having made her, keeps her oiled and steamed and going. God is master of nature's laws, but the only way we can keep from being crushed is to keep out from under her wheels. This is possible for a while; we can weather the gales, we can stem the storms, we can escape the earthquakes and the plagues and throttle the diseases which would prey upon us, for a while; but as certainly as man is born, he dies. He must be caught somewhere in the machinery sooner or later. All the forces exact their toll. They that go down to the sea in ships pay toll out of their number; so do those who toil at their work, and those who sleep in their houses. They that are struck by lightning die; they that sink into the sea drown; they that fall from high houses are killed; they that are taken with consumption waste away; they that practice sin pull through life with a quivering conscience and drop into the drakness of eternal night. All these laws are immutable, and no one need look to nature for clemency, or call upon the Governor of the universe to make an exception in his case.

Man as a sinner is subject to the laws that be, and he is under them. He may successfully ride the turning timbers of vicissitude as they float down the stream of time; but he is sure of the whirlpool when his journey ends, at the cataract, where the stream of time plunges into the ocean of eternity.

Indeed, when we are acquainted with that law by which sin transfers its subject from life to death, the wonder is that Adam lived so long after he sinned in Eden, and that our days on earth, with gladness interspersing our sorrows, and sunshine intervening our shadows, are so long extended. Did not God say to Adam, "In the day that thou eatest thereof thou shalt surely die?" Is it any less true today? Why is it that the ax of execution, hanging over the sinner's head, does not drop and cut him off, according to the law; for it is a law, a divine law, a natural law; and its fulfillment is due to come true as promptly as the breaking of the criminal's neck follows the falling of the hangman's trap. He that sins is his own hangman, under distributive justice. What hand holds the trap that its falling is delayed? And may not the hand that can thus delay the inevitable prevent the inevitable? Nay, since I have found that He can, and that for all who follow Him, He does, let me go further with my interesting search and ask how, and by what process does God, who cannot lie, who has seen best to ordain that the wages of sin be death, obviate the enforcement upon my guilty soul of a law which is as immutable as the Creator's throne.

Zaleucus of the seventh century B. C. was one of the earliest compilers of Grecian law. He became ruler of a Greek colony in southern Italy, for which he was lawgiver, as it was a miniature nation. The penalty for a certain sin was blindness. Soon after this law was made, the son of Zaleucus was arrested and convicted of this crime, and the people requested the good ruler to make an exception and not put out the eyes of his son. It was his impulse as a father to spare the son, but the public welfare demanded the enforcement of the law, and as a ruler, Zaleucus could not exempt the young man. There were in the breast of this ruler two motives which were so nearly irreconcilable that it required desperate measures for them to abide together. One was the motive of a father, the other was the motive of a king. The sacrifice of the one motive involved a sentence upon a much loved son; the sacrifice of the other endangered the welfare of the government. Zaleucus could do neither, he would do neither, and he did neither. Then, what did he do? Stepping down from his tribunal he ordered his executioner to strike out one of his own eyes, and one of his son's eyes. The integrity of the government was maintained, the son was saved from the force of the penalty, and both the ruler and his son carried a scar which proclaimed that justice and mercy had met together, and that by some marvelous process which only love could seek out, neither justice nor mercy had sacrificed its character.

If we let this erring son represent sinners and the ruler represent God, let us hunt for the scars. Look for the final word picture of Jesus Christ, and you will find nail prints in His hands; similar marks will appear in His feet; look again, and you will see in His side the mark of a wound made by that famous spear-thrust when they removed Him from the cross. Much is made of these scars in the inspired writings; and no doubt the redeemed of all ages will look upon them as an eloquent memorial of the day when mercy and truth met together and righteousness and peace kissed each other—the day when the everlasting permanency of the divine government was reaffirmed, and the boundless love of God for man was emphasized. As for us, our scars are not hard to find. Sin has born its fruit in pains, maladies, wounds, disappointments, poverty, sorrow and death; and the most penitent and pious have nevertheless carried the scars and paid these temporary penalties. But our illustration is not at all exact in what it sets forth. The proportion of penalty borne by the son of Zaleucus does not represent the proportion of the penalty for our sins which we bear. That penalty which we suffer is only the local and incidental consequences of sin, which in the nature of the case cannot even be equitably divided among us. The evening up does not come this side of the sinner's future state of perdition. The division of the penalty which our Lord makes with us provides that it shall be practically all His; and to all lawful and governmental ends, it is all His; "Jesus paid it all." "The sufferings of this present time are not worthy to be compared with the glory that shall be revealed in us;" and when we calculate that every anguish and hardship of life that is worthily assumed works out for us a far more exceeding and eternal weight of glory, we have to decide that God so regarded the completeness of Christ's ransom that He jealously gave Him all the credit for the redemption, neutralizing what little penalty we bear here by reimbursing us proportionately in the world to come.

CHAPTER IX.

THE INTERMEDIATE STATE.

We use the term intermediate state because it is in use, being understood to refer to a man in that period between the death and the resurrection of his body. That there was also an intermediate place, where the souls of the righteous should abide between death and the resurrection was the interpretation of Old Testament teachings by the more pious Jews prior to the time of Christ. They used the word paradise with reference to such a place, though this word had a broader employment, and it has a still broader use to-day. The accurate religious use of the word paradise will no doubt make it a synonym for heaven, and it seems clear that the Lord used it in this sense when he comforted the pardoned thief on the cross. There is not sufficient ground to hold that two separate places are provided for man in his two modes of existence after this life. It is quite apparent that the soul of Stephen went to the abode of his Lord. Acts 7:56, 60. If the home of disembodied saints must be different from the home of those clothed in their glorified bodies, then the abode of Enoch and Elijah, and of our Lord and of the few honored saints who arose at his resurrection must be separate from that of all other redeemed ones who have been gathered to their fathers. This is hardly to be presumed. Angels are not carnate beings; a different order from man, but the mode of existence with an angel and the soul of a man must be identical; yet heaven is suited for angels. May it not be as well suited for the souls of the departed saints? If it is suited for them, the thought of a separate place under the name of paradise is gratuitous.

There is hardly a doubt that the body of Moses was sleeping in the dust at the time of Christ's transfiguration. The record says he died, and God buried him. There is no room to assume that he had been raised from the dead, for the inspired writer specifically says that Christ became the firstfruits of them that slept; this cuts us off from assuming that anybody, prior to Christ's resurrection, had been raised from the dead into a glorified body. Yet on the mount of transfiguration we see the trio, representing the three modes of human existence. Jesus in mortal flesh; Elijah in his translated body; Moses without the body. That they are all together today is the most wholesome idea of heaven. True it may be, and probably is, that Moses was among the number of saints who arose with Jesus, and walked the streets of Jerusalem after his resurrection; but we will have to manufacture grounds to say that Moses and Elias were not together prior to this, that they came to the mount of transfiguration from different directions. The materialists could solve this for us if we had time to listen to their solution, by telling us that Moses and Elijah were not really present at the transfiguration, but that Peter and John (and Jesus) had a vision of them; but this would create the absurd condition of Jesus speaking in an apostrophe. If we were put to the task of proving such things as the real presence of Moses and Elias on the mount of transfiguration we would never get through wasting time on quibbles.

Jesus is in heaven, in his glorified body. None but the rank infidel disputes that. The Christian acceptance of the Scriptures leads us to conclude that Paul had inspired insight and was infallibly correct when he said that for him to be absent from the body would mean for him to be present with the Lord. The old hero loved his work, and counted it a privilege for him to toil and suffer for the Master. He was loath to turn loose the gospel plow; he said, "I am in a strait betwixt two;" to live would be Christ, but to die would be gain, for he would be in the immediate presence of his Lord. Nor was he to be disappointed. The strife is done, and he is there today. One cruel drop of Nero's ax, a spattering of consecrated blood, the quivering of a tired body, and all was over; the work of a chosen vessel was done; the time of his anchor lifting had come, and he was off, across seas of ether, to his heavenly home. Today the ashes of the honored expounder of the doctrine of the resurrection rest in the city of Rome, awaiting the last trump, for the trump shall sound; and he, the lover of the unlovely, the friend of the pagan, our toiling, self-sacrificing spiritual parent, our immortal benefactor, is with his Lord.

CHAPTER X.

THE MILLENNIUM.

A candid writer of a book bearing the title of this could not well ignore the subject of the Millennium, though this is more appropriately the future of the world than the future of man. Scripture passages applied to this subject are usually of uncertain application, and capable of various interpretations. Too much emphasis upon it tends to materialism and diverts the believer's mind from the thought of that city which hath foundations, whose builder and maker is God. Not for a moment would we tolerate the untenable theory that this earth is to be the eternal heaven of all redeemed mankind. We would about as soon try to prove that the heart of the earth were hell. Heaven was an existing fact when this planet became fallen. It was an existing fact when Enoch and Elijah took their exit from this world; and when Jacob spent the night at Bethel. Stephen, before his death, saw into its open portal, Paul heard the language of its inhabitants, and many a dying saint has been met by its light and greeted by its hosts. We have no differences to split with materialism. It is true that John saw the heavenly Jerusalem, coming down from God, and it is evident that his vision was of the real thing —a city, with a river, with trees, streets, and measurable walls; but his expression, "I saw (it) coming down," was not to be taken literally, since it referred to a city that cannot be moved; the vision was all that came to him.

The theory of a physical reign of departed saints a thousand years in the bodily presence of Christ upon this earth is based upon one obscure passage of Scripture (Rev. 20), which does not positively say that these saints shall have risen from the dead, or that the reign shall be upon earth, or that it shall be direct and literal. It is very possible that this passage refers to an event entirely separate from that good age of the world which the prophets foretell, which we have learned to call the millennium, and which, if we do not misunderstand the Scriptures, is to be inaugurated about the time of the second coming of Christ. It seems from the trend of Revelation, and the setting of that passage that the thousand years represent the period of the general Judgment, and it is not improbable that the allusion to the beheaded saints means that they were raised, and stood conspicuous and honored among the assembled hosts around the judgment bar, as the dead, small and great, were standing before God, and the books were being opened.

So far as the "first resurrection" is concerned, we are not warranted in saying that it here refers to order; *first* may refer to quality, and correspond with the term "better resurrection," in Hebrews 11:35; for all the holy have part in it, yet it is evident that Jesus had taught Mary that the resurrection of the saints should be at the last day. John 11:24. It is true that order is referred to in two other passages, namely 1 Cor. 15:23, 24, and 1 Thess. 4:16; but the former deals with the order of Christ and His people, and the latter simply states that the dead in Christ shall rise first—before we which are alive and remain shall be gathered up. The question of whether there will be one or two resurrections in point of time is not worth contending over. Maybe the righteous will rise first, but we see no particular reason why they should, as all are to be separated and judged together; and, if the resurrections are to be separate, the principal references to the resurrection do not attach enough importance to this detail to mention it; see, for instance, Daniel 12:2 and John 5:28, 29.

The prophets give to us a very pretty picture of an age of righteousness and peace, when the knowledge of the Lord shall cover the earth as the waters cover the sea, when the desert shall blossom as the rose, when ferocious animals shall no longer prowl the forests, and all the serpents that remain shall be harmless pets; when holiness to the Lord will be the watchword, an imprint and token of genuineness and equity upon the commonest manufactured utilities. In short the Wicked one shall have disappeared from the earth; 2 Thess. 2:8. And just here is a key that will explain how all this is to come to pass; both gradually and instantaneously; the sum of it will be an achievement of the Lord Jesus Christ. Speaking of that Wicked one, the writer says, "Whom the Lord shall consume with the spirit (or breath) of His mouth, and shall destroy with the brightness of His coming." This certainly means that the world's millennium will follow an age of moral and religious progress and improvement, and finally come in by an epoch, the second coming of Christ. The Bible and the preached and exemplified word represent the breathings of Christ on earth, and these agencies are working among the nations, to elevate mankind and diminish diabolism and the power of Satan. Most marvelously have they worked through the Christian centuries. While millions have been sent on to the New Jerusalem through the instrumentality of the gospel, its leaven has worked wholesale improvement among the nations of earth. In all the ages of

Chaldean, Egyptian, and Chinese history they had no age of progress to be compared with that of the nations in the last few centuries, where the gospel of Christ has been published. They went to a high state of pagan civilization, but it was by thousands of years of plodding; and public conscience and private ethics were by common consent exceedingly crude. Moreover, they reached a limit over which they could not pass, and then began to drag downward to a miserable depth. The prophecy with regard to Christian civilization—that civilization in which the leaven of the gospel is at work—is that it will reach no altitude beyond which it cannot rise, and though about the time of the final restitution there will be a lapse, around the edges, as it were (Rev. 20:7-9), the inroads of Satan upon the redeemed commonwealth will never be serious, and there will be no lasting decline.

Our Lord is today breathing upon the nations and reducing the evils of the world. Some brethren maintain the opposite as to the decline of evil, but, whether they are conscious of the fact or not, their contention, being without corroboration in history or foundation in Scripture, is for the sake of a dogma relating to the second coming of Christ. They have not seen where they could dispense with the contention and remain premillennialists, though they could do it; and to dispense with this notion would add much to a wholesale optimism, and more intelligent missionary and evangelistic motives.

The kingdom is coming; the leaven is working; there is a march of progress which if we had eyes to see would add new joy to our lives. The readers of prophecy who see great scare crows ahead have fallen short in their interpretations. Those who imagine that mediaeval Romanism is destined to menace our free government; that capital and labor have not the resources to adjust their differences without mutual destruction, that there is not sufficient balm in Gilead for the race troubles, that monopolies and trusts are destined to be the ultimate masters of civilization, that the Orient will combine against the Occident in annihilating wars, have simply borrowed trouble and crossed bridges that will never be built. Of course there will be a few wars along, and the material reduction of armament may be deferred for many years. Of course there will be race friction, as the lower strata of humanity struggle, under the stimulus of the Christian spirit, to rise. Business methods will be abused, and capital and labor will have many peaceful and a few sanguine struggles for what they claim to be their rights. Mediaeval Romanism is gradually fading, and an institution of another character is slowly but surely taking its place. The breasts of all mankind are being filled with a spirit which assures the impossibility of papal usurpation, and Jesuitism in its rank form is ashamed of its own countenance.

Traceable plainly to the spirit of Jesus is a large number of reforms. Public conscience, which means our ideal for others, never knew such a quickening as it is undergoing today. Such things as lotteries, pugilism, oppressive combines, gambling, traffic in impure foods, intoxicants, and drugs that menace society, things which were allowed to resolve themselves, under old regimes, things many of which did not conflict with the ethical and economical standards of yesterday, are being outlawed today. The day of slavery is over. The day of peonage is passing. Prisons are being reformed. Hospitals and asylums are dotting the land. Human life is held more sacred, and the common man is a greater quantity. Duels as a mode of settling differences between men of honor belong to the relics of barbarism; courts of arbitration and peace councils are common, and many a conflict is averted. The savagery of international warfare is reduced by the regultations of an international court. The gospel of the Prince of Peace is making inroads upon darkened nations so rapidly that a man has to keep his eyes wide open to keep track of the new achievements of the gospel in heathen lands, and to keep acquainted with the new champions of missionary enterprise who are every year coming upon the stage.

Let not the dissenting school misunderstand us. Some may think to quote 2 Peter 3:3, 4, as a response to this chapter: "There shall come in the last days scoffers, walking after their own lusts, and saying, Where is the promise of his coming? for since the father's fell asleep, all things continue as *they were* from the beginning of the creation." But we are not scoffers, we walk not after our own lusts, and we see the promise of His coming, not only in the Bible, but in all the signs of the times. All things do not continue as they were. As the day draws nearer the light shines brighter and the strength of His ancient enemy wanes upon the earth. We would not be guilty of crying peace when there is no peace; we do not think of pacifying a nation or a people in their sins, and this nation and people have many sins. We do not hold that the general reforms, influenced by the leaven of the kingdom, prove that a majority or even a large multitude of individuals are saved from their sins and ready for heaven. We fear they are not. There is need of a great spiritual awakening everywhere. There is need of individual workers to persuade people everywhere to receive Christ for their personal salvation. A great outpouring of the Spirit is needed in all the churches; but the best way for us to accomplish this is not by a depressing misinterpretation of prophecy and a habitual bemoaning of the fortunes of the world. This is not conducive to religious joy, yet the joy of the Lord in our hearts is an essential, if we would teach transgressors His ways, and cause sinners to be converted unto Him. The man who wins souls is the one on whom the sun shines. Perfect love hopeth all things.

The ideal age of the world will be the last age, before the final consummation of all things. With all the general improvements there will be much lack of faith at the coming of Christ, much neglect of personal salvation, and many of the very stewards of the Lord living and working out of the divine order. There will be some intense types of ungodliness, despite the glaze of a God-given civilization. A class called evil men and seducers will become more intense, more artful in vice and deception, and more set in their ways. The coming of Christ, which the Scriptures uniformly teach us is to judge the world, will finally destroy this wickedness.

It will be remembered that the judgment is to be a period, not a mere twenty-four hour day; that it is to be somewhere in the elements, where the throne of God will be the gravitative center. It is not improper to suppose that during this period things will continue upon the earth, and Christian civilization will have reached its climax; that this will be the millennium; that at the close of the judgment period, be it a thousand years, or more, or less, those still living, having been preceded by the dead in Christ, shall be changed and judged, following a brief period of lapse in which Satan shall have renewed his energies against the splendid civilization of the last days—then the consummation, and eternity, no part of which is yet delineated to us by Him who designs the future of the creatures He has made in His image.

CHAPTER XI.

THE GENERAL RESURRECTION.

The resurrection of the body is a mystery, says the apostle; a phenomenon among the forces which the laws with which we are acquainted cannot explain. The Greeks were gifted in explaining things, and whatever was unfathomable to them was foolish. They received Paul's sermon very well at Athens till he spoke of the resurrection of the dead; then, "Some mocked: and others said, We will hear thee again of this matter." We have a great many Greeks today among Christian scholars. Our modern educators have drank at the fountains of Hellen and digged among the ancient ruins of a civilization which Providence folded away to give place to a better testament, till the mantel of those polished rationalists has fallen upon them, and, with all its capacity and incapacity, the spirit of Greek wisdom has preempted their minds. If some of the present day writers upon the resurrection could drop back nineteen centuries and be transferred to Mars hill they could preach a sermon on the resurrection which would please the Greek philosophers and add to the glamour of St. Paul's unpopularity at the Areopagus.

The subject of the resurrection has a wide place in both the Old and New Testaments. In the early apostolic preaching it was made prominent, as if they regarded it a necessary element in a well rounded faith; and, so far were they from carelessness in regard to the subject that they suffered much opposition which would not have come, had they consented to remain silent upon this hope-inspiring subject.

That our body shall be raised a spiritual body is set over against the fact that it shall be sown a natural body (1 Cor. 15:44); and what the one means ought to be easily determined, when we ascertain the meaning of the other. A natural body is a body hedged about by what we call natural laws and conditions, and subject to them. It is a body that may be hurt by a blow; that may be drowned or burned; that may get sick or tired; that may grow old or wear out; that is subject to gravity and dependent on the ordinary vehicles of locomotion; it is a member of a race that must eat and sleep, and may propagate its kind. These and others are the attributes of a natural body which we are allowed to presume do not belong to a body which is not subject to natural laws, but which is passed into another realm of government and sensation. How many of the attributes of a spiritual or immortal body are held in common with a natural body we are not in position to determine.

The apostle plainly teaches that this immortal body is raised out of the ashes of the buried mortal. He does not claim that the exact chemical atoms will be cast anew; the chemical atoms of many a body have been scattered abroad, passing into vegetation and into the formation of other bodies, but this does not interfere with Paul's theory of the resurrection. He purposely discusses (1 Cor. 15) the plastic quality in the hand of God of those elements out of which flesh is composed, where he speaks of the different kinds of flesh, and of the bodies celestial and terrestrial. While there may not be much change in the chemical proportions of the body, it is believed upon pretty good evidence that the material of the body changes completely about every seven years. There is of course a change in the relation of the atoms of the body to one another at different times in life, so that we may say that as age comes on the relation of the atoms of the body become strained. It has been held with good show of reason that the formation of the body is a product of the soul; that the soul clothes itself in the years allotted for physical growth, and that it is the designer of its own costumes in all absolutely normal cases. The consistency of this view appears in the fact that two boys of identical physical heredity may be led into opposite pursuits, or kinds of education, or one into good habits and pious ways and the other into bad habits and infidel meditations and it will affect their features, and sometimes their entire physical form.

The *Baltimore Sun* quotes a chemist as estimating that all the constituents of a hundred and fifty-pound man are contained in 1,200 eggs. He said: "There is enough gas in a man to fill a gasometer of 3,649 cubic feet. There is enough iron to make four nails. There is enough fat to make 75 candles and a large cake of soap. There is enough phosphorous to make 8,064 boxes of matches. There is enough hydrogen in him to fill a balloon and carry him up to the clouds. The remaining constituents of a man would yield, if utilized, six cruets of salt, a bowl of sugar and ten gallons of water."

With such a form as a man has made for himself, out of the grave where his ashes lie, God proposes to clothe again the soul that is in hades, and this is the resurrection; only the glory of the righteous and the shame of the wicked is to be enhanced, because of the transparency of their immortal bodies, out of which their characters, good or bad, shall shine as through a lens.

But suppose that we or any other writer have poorly delineated the idea of the resurrection; suppose that much we hold proves speculative, under better light; suppose that our plea for it, as has been the case with some, has weakened our cause; it remains that the dead, small and great, shall rise; that those in the graves shall hear the voice of God; and no figurative theory, or germ theory; or trichotomy theory, can meet the specifications of Scripture. The presence of mystery in the doctrine is admitted, though, as the apostle says, it is no greater than the mystery attending a grain of corn which perishes today to be succeeded by many grains of like composition, merging from the same grave in a few months. The apostle had not the remotest idea of teaching by this illustration the foolish theory that every human body possesses an imperishable germ; but rather, by an illustration which was incidentally in the neighborhood of analogous, he sought to impress the inquirer that mysterious things obtain and are demonstrated before our eyes, where no human law can explain the mystery, and that we should not question the ability of God who takes the chemicals of earth and makes new corn over the grave of the old, to clothe our soul in an immortal body on the resurrection morning.

CHAPTER XII.

THE JUDGMENT.

We are responsible beings; a consciousness of this is native in us. A man must answer for his behavior here; and according to the Scriptures, he must answer in an open court. The grounds of every sentence must be stated in plain terms, and we are taught that a representative multitude of mankind shall witness the evidence and hear the Judge as He reviews the case and pronounces the sentence. The Scriptures continually enforce upon us the thought that this universe is under a stated government, that its Ruler knows all things, and that the penalty for the violation of His laws is infallible, not to be evaded by technicalities, not to be confused by shrewd attorneys; that no case will under any circumstances need to be remanded for a new trial, and that the deserts of no one will be doubtful. The Judge will not be perplexed over any character, as we are sometimes in doubt, but will readily give His reasons for an adverse or a favorable sentence as the names are called. Having made man a rational being, God proposes to recognize the right of man to understand the terms of every sentence.

The Hereafter. 59

That God knows now the deserts of every one, and that every soul at death passes immediately to his reward might make it difficult, at a glance, to see the reason for a general judgment; but the fact that God has ordained that such a thing shall be is to us sufficient, even if we could not comprehend a reason. But a reason seems not far to seek: If God is pleased to outline before a representative jury the reason for every sentence, to review the lives of the people, it is necessary that a period next to the final consummation should be set apart for this purpose. Every government has its court week. If with reference to every life there must be a revelation, if for the righteous there must be a formal vindication, we can see why God hath appointed a day in which to judge the world (Acts 17:31). We are taught that "God shall bring every work into judgment, with every secret thing, whether it be good or whether it be evil"; that "we must all appear before the judgment seat of Christ."

As suggested in Chapter IV., a stitch has been dropped in the plan of God. From the day that the stitch was dropped, God set on foot agencies to recover it, and bring things back like they ought to be. This could not be done in a moment, without intercepting some events which might be of great importance to the universe. It could not be done, even gradually, without great sacrifice, and we do not know that in the economy of divine government it would have been possible completely to recover the lapse in a few days. But after all, a few thousand years are with God not more than a few days, and millions of years from now, when we look back, though we will still be impressed with the gravity of the fall and the importance of these few years of probation, the period of disorder will seem but a span. The day of judgment, instead of being the first day of eternity I should prefer to say will be the last day of time. It is a part of God's process in the restoration. It would seem that He has chosen to divide the restoration period into two days—the day of gospel and the day of judgment; taking the word day to mean a period, which it often does, in history and in prophecy. By the gospel period we do not mean merely the Christian era, but we use the term in its broader sense, to embrace all the centuries in which God is found inviting man to be saved by faith in Him, from the days of righteous Abel till the end of the days of grace, which, during the millennium, according to the solution which we have suggested, will overlap the judgment period.

The judgment, then, as well as the gospel, is

one of God's methods in effecting the restitution, the gospel being the better, and hence being allowed a long tenure. The gospel method is suasive and the judgment method is compulsory. The gospel method saves all that attend upon it, the judgment method damns all who, rejecting the gospel method, wait for it. All that can be won are won, then comes judgment, and the rest are forced; but since no one can be forced into an acceptable service of God, all that wait till judgment must bow the knee and die.

All differences must be adjusted; all debts must be settled; all who have sinned in secret must be found out, and the treachery and injustice of the cruel and the unjust must overtake them. It is the property of judgment to see that all this is done.

Before that tribunal must appear every being that is fallen or that has ever been fallen, that the one class may be formally and forever dismissed from the presence of God, and that the recovery of the other class may be ratified and confirmed. Even the angels that kept not their first estate are reserved in everlasting chains unto the judgment of that great day.

In the judgment period the physical universe shall be called upon, as the revelator saw it, to emphasize in the presence of a rational universe the terribleness of sin and the dreadfulness of God. The stars shall fall from heaven as a fig tree casteth her untimely figs when she is shaken of a mighty wind; the moon shall be turned to a clot of blood, and a crepe of blackness shall be spread over the face of the sun. The earth shall reel under the tread of the judgment host; the sea shall heave and belch forth her sleeping multitudes. The graveyards shall cleave asunder, the tombs shall scatter and the dead, small and great, shall stand before God. It shall be then as if there were no atonement—there will be none—the days of grace will be ended. The doves of mercy and love which formerly had perched upon our premises and rested at our fire sides will have spread their wings and sought retreat behind the throne of a just God. Not a star of hope will shine throughout all the dark firmament; and on every side there will be no representative of God—but sheriffs of justice. Altars will fall! Sanctuaries, no longer needed by an unworthy race, will be cast down; angry lightnings will play abroad, and muttering thunders will announce to trembling men and angels that God is a God of absolute justice, true to His word, and that it is a fearful thing to sin and fall into His hands.

CHAPTER XIII.

HELL.

There is not any room to doubt that Jesus taught the doctrine of the future punishment of the wicked, and it appears that He dwelt upon the subject, not as a theme which He enjoyed, but as a necessary warning, a primary element in the doctrine of repentance. At the close of one of His severest messages on the wrath of God (Matt. 23) the mood of the Teacher is shown in the fact that He weeps and utters those words so celebrated for tenderness, beginning, "O, Jerusalem, Jerusalem."

It appears evident that in all the centuries since the ministry of Jesus the regular churches have held consecutively the view that they now hold concerning the future punishment of the wicked, and that it does not materially differ from what Jesus taught. We hold that what He taught was infallibly correct, even if it should fail to tally with our sentiments and deductions.

There cannot be law without penalty. Men are not paying the penalty for their sins in this world. It is true that suffering frequently follows sin, quickly; but often this is not the case.

It is true that the way of transgressors is hard; but in this world there are exceptions even to this rule, while, in a temporal sense, righteous people sometimes suffer much and have a hard time on account of the doings of the wicked. It does not take a very smart man to see, apart from the Bible, that on the hypothesis of a divine law, which must carry a divinely prescribed penalty, there must be a future punishment. Then when we consult the Bible on the subject, we are repeatedly assured, in language which must be understood, that there is a future punishment for the ungodly.

It will not be out of place for us to glance briefly at the philosophy of this punishment. First of all we would observe that it is a natural result of sin. While it may not be the immediate result, it is the final and inevitable. Someone once asked a preacher to locate hell for him, and the preacher said, Sir, hell is located at the end of a sinner's earthly life. And why is punishment the consequence of sin? Why did not a great and good Creator make His laws of cause and effect to operate in another direction? We answer, it would have been against His government if His intelligences could have sinned with impunity. Under the economy of the universe, which we are too finite to criticise, and which, if we were less finite we would not want to criticise, punishment is a necessity—hell is a necessity. God has myriads who possess the capacity of monarchs; and they must be impressed that it is an awful thing to sin against Him.

Driven, as all reasonable men must be, face to face with the fact of future punishment, our first impulse will be to inquire into the character of this punishment.

First of all we would notice that it must be a state of unspeakable wretchedness and anguish, for it is set in antithesis to heaven. If heaven is a high place hell is called the low place. If heaven is a city whose gates stand open forever, and where it is perpetual day, hell is a pandemonium where night reigns. For the joys of heaven we have the sighings of hell, for the angels of heaven, we have the devils of hell, and for the fruition of hope on one hand, we have the culmination of despair on the other. We do not think it is necessary for us to insist on any particular form of punishment in hell; it is enough for us to say that hell is the opposite of heaven. The many figures of speech, such as a dark night, a troubled sea, or a lake of fire, are given to convey to our dull perception the dreadfulness of that awful world from which God has hidden his face.

Another startling and overwhelming truth

about this future punishment is that it is eternal. To this, many people take exceptions; and we will respectfully notice their objections in the proper place.

The two chief and sufficient evidences that future punishment is eternal are the following:

1. Man is an eternal being. He is possessed of natural immortality. When God breathed life into his body man became an immortal soul. This immortality is a fact of consciousness in every well-adjusted man. This consciousness was corroborated by the great Teacher, who assumed that man had a soul (Matt. 16:26) using the word soul in the sense we here use it, as the immortal part of man. He brought immortality to light, says Paul, one of His chief expounders. And Paul himself expressed his consciousness of this immortality, and his inspired knowledge of it, when he said that at the death of his body he would depart and be with Christ (in heaven). Peter also expressed this as his understanding of Christ's doctrine of immortality, and John in his apocalyptic vision saw the souls of them whose bodies had been decapitated and were still sleeping in the dust. In treating a soul as immortal Jesus made no difference between the righteous and the wicked, really having more to say about the perpetuation of consciousness in the wicked af-

ter their physical death. If you couple the fact of man's natural immortality with the fact that his disease of sin is incurable, and that it is a soul disease, you have the first and primary established proof of eternal punishment. There is a time when by one exclusive remedy, Christ's blood of atonement, a soul may be recovered from its disease of sin, but there is hardly any one who doubts that an intelligence may finally get beyond the reach of this remedy. Not that the remedy is lacking in infinite power, but there comes a time with a sinner when the die is cast; when there is nothing in him to respond to a call of mercy; when there remains in him not a single aspiration to righteousness. There may be only a few who have crossed the dead line in this world, but no doubt there are a few, and all sinners certainly will have done so, when they pass into eternity. Man's tendency is a proof of the possibility that he may become hopelessly incorrigible; and such a creature, having reached such a state, if he lives forever must suffer forever.

2. The inspired Book of God takes the position that future punishment is eternal. Repeatedly does it indicate this fact, but one passage, the most inspired of the inspired, is sufficient; the words of Jesus: "These shall go away into everlasting punishment, but the right-

eous into life eternal." Matt. 25:46. In the original Greek, the word used for the duration of blessedness in this verse is exactly the same as that used for the duration of future punishment. Indeed it is the same word as is elsewhere used to indicate how long God is to live.

There are three objections to the doctrine of future and eternal punishment which we will account worthy to be considered. One assumes to be a scriptural objection, one is sentimental, and one assumes to be a philosophical objection.

1. It is held that where the Scriptures speak of the destruction of the wicked, and where other similar language is used, it means their annihilation. But let it be remembered that *destruction* and *annihilation* are far from being synonyms. While annihilation means to resolve into nothing, destroy means to unbuild, so that the thing that was once glorious is in ruins, and that which was once useful is useless and abandoned. The meaning of death in such expressions as "the second death" is somewhat similar. It may or may not involve the demise and unconsciousness of the body, but it always involves the conscious wretchedness of the soul.

2. It is held that the sufferings of hell are not consistent with what we know to be God's attributes of goodness and power. This ob-

jection, if it holds good at all, does not touch the question of the eternity of hell; for if it is inconsistent, it would be as logically inconsistent for a century as for eternity. We are witnesses to the fact that suffering does exist. The world is full of it today, and has been for thousands of years. In hospitals and asylums, in cities and country places, in homes of rich and poor, and on land and sea. Hearts are aching; bodies are racked with pain; multitudes are wrung with mental anguish;—a mother, because a daughter is gone down in shame; a companion, because of the infidelity of a companion; a widow, because her staff of support is gone and the world is treating her cruelly; an orphan, because the light of home and parental love have been extinguished, and the burdens of life are heavy. Here comes the black bordered letter; the sad telegram; the sudden tragedy, or the days of sickness, and the black box. There is sorrow in the palace, there is anguish in the slums, there is trouble on the farm; a flood has drenched a city; an earthquake has enveloped a land with misery; a storm has swept away the people's homes, bringing desolation and death. There is no end of suffering, there is no bound too it, and its volume cannot be measured; yet God lives, He sees it all, and He is infinitely good and powerful. Can you understand that? No, no more than you can understand the sufferings of hell; not so well; yet you have to accept it, for you are facing it. We say you cannot understand it so well. There is more mystery attending earthly suffering, for it is so unevenly distributed, and there are many of whom it can be said, Neither did this man nor his parents sin, that he should suffer. Things are constituted so that oppressors have grown fat upon the oppressed; the innocent often suffer the penalty of the misdoings of the guilty, and the guilty in many cases go apparently without suffering. But how different the sufferings of hell! No innocent feet walk its dark corridors. No defenseless widows suffer from the heartlessness of wicked men; no godly mothers and fathers sit in the gloom with bleeding hearts and bewail miseries which they did not bring upon themselves; no innocent man lies crushed and bleeding from accidents due to the faults of others; no hungry orphans cry for bread and suffer from the abuses of the cruel. Thus are the sufferings of hell more easily explained than the sufferings of earth, and hence more thinkable, in the abstract. The inhabitants of another world who would betake themselves to a study of human suffering if you should hand them a text book upon the sufferings of hell and one upon the sufferings of

The Hereafter.

earth, would find it much easier to master the philosophy of the former than of the latter; and if they were inclined to be skeptical about one of the text books it would be that relating to earth; not that the one relating to earth would describe punishment so severe and universal, but because it would depict the anguish of so many innocent sufferers. The sufferings of earth therefore teach us that the sufferings of hell can be.

Sentimental students have widely mistaken the character of God. His attributes represent a full circle; He fulfills every office, whether it require a touch that is infinitely delicate, a stroke that is firm, or a thrust that is severe. Not only is He the God that planted the lilies, made the zephyrs, taught the birds to sing and put the twinkle in the stars and the azure in the skies; He made the stormy ocean and the whirling tempest. The winds and waves obey His will and the flames are His servants. He made man, and to Him belongs the prerogative of death. As truly as His mercy is a healing balm, His justice is a glittering sword; as truly as He is the Father of the righteous, He is the King of the universe; as truly as He is the Savior of them that believe, He is the Judge of quick and dead. We are taught to fear Him with a wholesome fear, and certainly we must expect to find something in Him to fear, else the lesson would be an idle one.

3. It has been suggested that suffering could not be for an extended length of time; that man would become deadened and indifferent even to the punishment of hell; but it is the immortal that suffers in hell, and the immortal does not lose sensibility like the mortal, whether it be the sensibility of pleasure or pain. A law which would make one indifferent to extended pain would make him indifferent to extended pleasure. Hence if an eternal hell cannot be fully realized, neither may an eternal heaven be fully realized. But we are in reach of this subject, and can examine it for ourselves. Ask the man of God if the pleasures of religion are a declining quantity. He will tell you that the joys of salvation are fresh every morning. The aged saint who leans upon his staff, experiences emotions that are many times richer than the pleasures of his early religious life, if he has proved true to his trust. The converse is true of the aged sinner. Who has not watched with horror the gatherings of the hell clouds in the life of a wicked man as age crept upon him. The most miserable vileness that I have ever seen was the vileness of an old soul after a life had been spent in sin. Nor was he deadened to his anguish. The grip of misery fastened

itself more consciously upon the man as the sun of his life went down. Nor will joys grow old in heaven, nor will sorrow grow old in hell. Could I be more happy! will be the shout of a soul when it first looks upon the fields of the second Eden and the streets of the New Jerusalem; but each thousand years will discover new sources of pleasure and consolation. How time must fly in heaven. I think that Saint Paul and Moses feel that they have been there scarcely a week! But is it not the reverse in hell? Do not the lost in that fathomless abyss discover new sources of horror and new things to remind them in their regrets as the centuries pass? The unmarked years must drag by with great tediousness.

CHAPTER XIV.

FUTURE REWARDS.

A reward is something that comes because of merit. An infant, redeemed by the blood of Christ, being saved, is received into heaven; it has an eternal home. What its future may be in the infinite universe of God remains for us to speculate. It cannot, however, be rewarded for anything that it has done in this world. But, we are taught in the Scriptures that aside from the fact that they are cleansed and qualified for heaven by the atoning blood, a great multitude of people are to receive a reward for the deeds done in the body.

The word reward is used in the Scriptures in both a good and an evil sense; but its prominent meaning has reference to blessing rather than punishment. We will here use it in this light. As we look upon the population of this world with its manifold grades of merit and demerit, it relieves us to know that the future distribution of rewards is to be undertaken by the omniscient God.

The Holy Spirit in inditing the Scriptures, has chosen to remain silent in regard to details when speaking of future rewards. We are given to understand that some rewards will be greater than others, when the Bible speaks of one star differing from another star in glory, and people being rewarded according to the deeds done in the body. The extent of our service in the Master's vineyard on earth is made the principal basis upon which our reward shall be estimated. Of course, not to speak of service, our suffering for Jesus' sake will enhance the glory that shall be revealed in us hereafter. Included in "the sufferings of this present time" are the bearing of the brunt of religious persecution, the sacrificing of luxuries and comforts for the good of others and for the promotion of Christ's kingdom, and the patient endurance of temporal hardships, obscurity and hamperings that fall to our portion.

Our sufferings may be classified under two general headings; we would place in one group that kind of suffering which more directly contributes to the spread of the kingdom of heaven and partakes of the nature of service in the Lord's vineyard; in the other group, we would place those sufferings which cannot, in their nature, edify any but the individuals who patiently endure them. Now, no human being is able to trace the boundary line between these two classes of suffering; for we may think that one who is bearing much affliction is only keeping himself, when the light of his Christlike patience radiates to inspire and bless a thousand others. Again, when we see some care-worn mother darning socks or mending little garments by lamp light, bending her form from day to day under the toil and confinement of a busy home life and shortening her days by spending anxous, sleepless nights, trying to reduce the fever and soothe the pain of some little sufferer, we say, "Poor woman;—much toil and little pay." We get the idea that her sphere is limited, and that, while her labor and fortitude will react favorably upon her own soul, she cannot be classed with such immortal sufferers as John Bunyan, whose suffering gave impetus to the spread of the kingdom, and that she will have no cumulative reward, because her sufferings do not take the nature of evangelical service, such as that rendered by St. Paul or John Wesley. But, we must remember that it was one of these same toiling, care-worn mothers that nourished St. Paul upon her breast, that rocked John Bunyan in his little cradle, and gave John Wesley his earliest impression. It is always possible that one who is toiling and suffering in perpetual obscurity, is touching some one else who will not only touch a nation or a continent, but who will touch several generations.

We now return to the statement that the extent of our service in the Master's vineyard on earth shall be the basis upon which our reward is estimated. "They that be wise shall shine as the brightness of the firmament; and they that turn many to righteousness, as the stars forever and ever." You remember that wisdom is the execution of knowledge; so that while knowledge is what we possess, wisdom is what we do. It is well therefore to reflect upon the fact that it is not they that have knowledge, but they that be wise that shall shine the brightest. No doubt this shining does not have reference to the mere outward appearance; it is rather a beautiful figure that relates to the magnitude of that reward which belongs to them whose lives have been full of diligent service.

I made mention of cumulative reward. Perhaps as I used liberty in appropriating this term, it would be well to dwell upon it a moment. We mean that which accumulates to a man's credit after the death of his body. The title of this chapter, "Future Rewards," applies not only to us who are still in the vineyard, but to the Christian fathers who we say have passed to their reward. They are only enjoying part of their reward now; much of it is *future*. How could you place to his credit all that is due St. Paul, or any other saint that started great movements, left examples and wrote books which are today doing more good than ever? It would be impossible unless the God of infinite foreknowledge should anticipate the result of their labors and pay them in advance. This He has not chosen to do, but has postponed the completing of all rewards until His coming, of which He says,"'Behold, I come quickly; and my reward is with me, to give every man according as his work shall be." The distribution of rewards will be involved with unlimited technicalities, but God can easily solve them all and give to every one his just deserts. It may be that some of your progeny in generations to come will be a light to them that sit in darkness, and the instrument for winning a million souls. If any faithfulness or diligence on your part has started a current that will help to produce this character, it will be placed to your credit on the account books up yonder. While the reward of the great evangelists of past centuries will not be ruduced in the least on this account, it is well understood that God will duly reward every one, no matter how remote, who had a part in producing those characters that have blessed the world.

Our future reward should be a chief stimulus in our trials and battles here below. The magnitude, the enduring splendor and the wholesome delight of this heavenly reward has perhaps never entered into the heart of man. Earthly pleasures fail, carnal joys lose their sweetness, a reward of glittering gold can be swept from our hands in a day; but the Master teaches that we may lay up treasures in heaven, where moth and rust do not corrupt, nor thieves break through and steal. Moses had respect to the recompense of his reward, and Paul said, "Henceforth there is laid up for me a crown."

God intends for the stimulating hope of an unspeakable reward in the next age to cause us to leave our earthly haunts of ease and self-seeking to save precious souls. The offer of these rewards is in itself an emphasis upon the inestimable value of an immortal soul. The question of one of our sweetest modern songs, "Will there be any stars in my crown?" should fire the heart of every soldier of Jesus Christ.

CHAPTER XV.

RECOGNITION IN HEAVEN.

Two kinds of normal love may and should dwell at once in the heart of man; the one a relative love, the other a benevolent love. With the former we love people according to their relationship to us or according to their loveliness. This love makes possible the organization of society into families, communions, and nations. With this love it is natural and right to love some better than others, and not to love at all in some cases. It was never intended that with the relative love faculty man should love his neighbor as himself, or love the heathen on the other side of the globe. But the heart is a vessel which can be full of both kinds of love at once, just as a vacuum can be filled at once with light and air, and the increase of one does not diminish the other. This other love of benevolence is little known by those not born of the Spirit, and not known in its completeness to any but those who are filled with the Spirit. With this love we love all alike; other people's families as well as our own. Mean people as well as good people; heretics as well as "kindred minds"; people whom we have not seen; the homely as well as the beautiful.

It is thus that we explain one problem in contemplating heaven. Some have advanced the barren and unwieldly thought that all of heaven's inhabitants will appear alike to us, and be equally dear; that a perfect society excludes relationships and groupings. But some basis for the grouping or districting of society, springing out of relative love, is necessary to the perfect organization of a commonwealth; and while the relationship of man and wife and of relative and relative shall not be defined there just as it is here, a relationship will certainly exist, and be preserved by a bond of relative affection. There is no reason and very little attraction in the thought that in heaven our loved ones will amount to no more than other people to us.

Arising from these thoughts, is the question of recognition in heaven. Recognition in heaven would not be an attractive subject were it not for the truth of the above observations. If relative love were only an earthly plant, it would be of little moment to an intelligent mind, whether he ever met his loved ones again. Individuality being practically blotted out, it would give him the same pleasure to meet some one of whom he never heard that it would to meet his own mother or child. This would add pathetic features to our parting at death, and would tend to discourage "natural affection" in this life, whereas the absence of natural affection is recognized by the apostle as nonconformity to heaven's laws, and a sign of great depravity.

We may think of a newly arrived soul in heaven as being very much like the unfallen Adam in Eden, with regard to mental attainments. Adam's mind faculties were perfect, though it would be absurd to think therefore that his knowledge was complete. He was capable of acquiring knowledge rapidly, but he had to acquire it. He had the thirst for knowledge which belongs to a normal mind, for it was of this that Satan took advantage when he tempted him to sin. A newly arrived soul in heaven will have brought with him all the true knowledge which he laboriously acquired upon the earth—small at best, limited in the smartest of men; related to our possible attainments in heaven something as a completed kindergarten course is related to the post-graduate studies of a university and all that comes between. Much of our knowledge when we arrive in heaven will have to be expunged or pruned. Either by means of perfect intuition we will instantly discard many of our former tenets of so-called knowledge, or else by our progressive discovery of facts in the case our knowledge will be sifted.

The infant will begin at the foundation of true knowledge. It may be supposed that everything in heaven is conducive to perfect development, and also to rapid development, in the primary or rudimentary principles of knowledge. The drudgery and mental travail necessary to progress here, may not be known there. Every exercise is pleasant in heaven.

The quality and color, and also the fulness, of our mental attainments, trace themselves upon the surface of our being in this life, and shall in the hereafter. It is therefore true that attainments or lack of attainments affect a man's personal appearance. For this reason, it is possible that our recognition of loved ones and former acquaintances in heaven may not be instantaneous, especially in a case where the loved one died in infancy. We may not know them, and it is certain that they cannot, by any natural method, know us. That might be true if one of our loved ones should spend many years in London or Paris, and we should visit them there. But though this may be true in the heavenly state, they will be no less our loved ones, when the acquaintance is made, and our natural affections, which represent an eternal faculty of the human soul, will be just as warm and pleasant as if we had been separated from them but a day.

CHAPTER XVI.

THE UNBRIDGED GULF.

There are certain substances in the material world which may be easily shaped into articles of utility while they are new, but which as they grow older become less plastic, until the time comes, finally, that they cannot be worked at all, when an effort to change them from what they are now into something else would simply involve their destruction. That is, their probationary period has passed; their day of grace has ended. There is full proof that this fact obtains among rational creatures, in the realm of heart and mind. You may follow man from the period of infancy till he is full of years, and at every stage you will notice evidence of a gradual fixing of character. When he is a little child he may be literally molded like wax, and marred as easily as molded. When he is a youth he may be carved like chalk, but the one who does the shaping finds that if his work is turned over to a spoiler it is soon undone. When he reaches young manhood he is like a soft stone, which must be chiseled into shape, but which holds its shape beautifully, though to smash the image is by no means impossible. Then it seems that the weather begins in earnest to harden the material, and every year reduces the probability that the image will ever be marred. Beyond the age of young manhood man passes through stage after stage in the hardening process, represented by the different kinds of workable stones found in the earth, till he becomes like that stone which the sculptor always avoids, because it yields not one particle of obedience to his splendid tools and his skillful strokes.

In the various stages after man passes a given period the value of the crude material goes down, because he ceases more and more to be available for the higher product of the sculptor's art. Thus we see that the soul of man grows less flexible and less plastic every year of his life, whether he be a good or a bad man; and there is no reason to doubt that this gradual fixing goes on till his character becomes an impregnable wall. Such is the character of Satan, unapproachable in darkness and depravity; such is the character of an angel of God, unapproachable in purity and light, and beyond the reach of seduction or contamination. And may it not be that some of the subjects of Satan reach that period of unapproachable darkness before they leave this world? And have we not seen some of the servants of God upon whose perseverance we could safely calculate, to whom that scripture applies which says, "He shall go no more out"?

One of the glories of heaven, an assurance that in the case of every inhabitant its bliss shall be eternal, is in that statement that "'there shall be no more curse"—no execration; nobody will change. It is this same property in man which fixes the eternity of hell. The limitation is not in God, but in man. The mercy of God is boundless and limitless; it endureth forever, apply it to whom you will; but when man passes the salvable stage he is eternally lost, whether he be in this or the other side of the river of Death. The gulf between the rich man and Lazarus was the same gulf that is between Gabriel and Satan, not measured by miles and leagues, but quite as real, and more impassable than if it were. It is a moral gulf; and moral distances, after they reach a certain limit, cannot be bridged even by infinity.

The 55th of Isaiah gives us the thought of a moral distance, where certain persons are represented as being near, but in danger of being farther, even out of hearing. The writer goes on to say that *returning* unto the Lord consists in abandoning the moral differences between the soul and God—"Let the wicked forsake his way, and the unrighteous man his thoughts: and let him return unto the Lord."

No bridge could be built across the gulf between Dives and Lazarus, but the bridge of the atonement in Jesus Christ spans the gulf between the sinner and God, until that sinner, continuing to neglect his eternal interests, fixes the difference between himself and his maker; the difference thus fixed, the love of God notwithstanding, the death of Christ in vain, the die is cast forever.

CHAPTER XVII.

THE ULTIMATE KINGDOM.

A kingdom is a government. When Jesus told his disciples that the kingdom of God was within or among them, he meant the government of God; that God was king, so far as they were concerned. In substance, then, the term kingdom of God, used in its various employments, means about the same, and an added adjective must relate chiefly to its extent of development. It is stages rather than kinds of kingdoms referred to, when the term finds different employments in religious literature.

They beheld only the shadows of the kingdom in the days prior to Moses, and with Moses came only the bare outline, to be imperfectly recognized in the commonwealth of Israel. With John the Baptist there came a voice saying, "The kingdom of heaven is at hand"; and under the ministry of Jesus Christ people of all nations began to long for citizenship and groan for naturalization.

Defined in the words of Paul, this kingdom has three fundamental properties; righteousness, peace and joy. The kingdom is made up of subjects, and these subjects furnish the setting for these three fundamental properties. It may be said of every one who resides in the kingdom of God that he is righteous, peaceful, joyful. The kingdom begins in the heart; it widens into a community, it is to spread to the nations, but it finds its highest representation in heaven above. Heaven above is simply a great government, where millions of subjects, under perfect divine control, with the law of God engraved in mind and affection, serve their King, and are free from every inward and outward inducement to treason or disloyalty.

Wherever you find it, the kingdom of God is a progressive force; it comes with power and it comes with subtlety, but it is always coming. It is "not of this world" in the sense that earthly weapons can bring it about. The most that we shall see of it in the world will not be at the close of a sanguine battle; yet it shall come, noiseless as the sun comes galloping over the hills in the morning, modestly as the rootlet breaks open the rock and puts forth into a tree with spreading foliage, generously as the leaven inflates the flattened dough cake into a liberal loaf.

Jesus Christ did not conceal his purpose to conquer the world. He said the Father had put the times and seasons in his own power, and we doubt not that the nature of the seasons is so wondrously concealed from us that we can hardlly detect the passing of their winters, springs, summers and autumns; yet the kingdom is coming, and "the seventh angel" is destined to say that the kingdoms of this world are become the kingdoms of our Lord and of his Christ. But he will have no need of their thrones nor of their palaces. His throne is already exalted, and the palaces of his servants, now under construction, will already be completed; it is the subjects of these kingdoms who shall become his. There is no mistaking the purpose of Christ. He gave us our weapons, mightier than swords, more invincible than battle ships; he puts in us the ideals which he would work out in the world, and bids us go to our task of producing the principles of his kingdom, in hearts, communities and nations. He permits us to use "all means in doing it, excepting means of violence and dishonor, the ballot, but not the sword; the platform, but not the whipping post; the school room, but not the bribe. Back of all, and permeating all, are prayer and the word of God.

The kingdom of God on earth, manifested through its subjects, is a practical working force. They claim the world for Christ; they stand without musket or sword and bravely deny all evil practices and traffics the right to exist on

The Hereafter.

the face of the earth. On yesterday it struck the death blow to slavery, on tomorrow it will finish the legalized liquor traffic, break up the intricate organizations of graft and uproot the white slave trade. Happy the thought; the kingdom of God is an inevitable force. It works while we sleep; it makes worth while the investment of our strength as disciples of Jesus Christ.

But what of the ultimate kingdom? The expression implies the coming of a day when there shall be nothing else to conquer; when there shall be no ambassadors, for there shall be no foreign ports; when there shall be no soldiers, for the fate of the rebellion shall be decided. Then we shall be forever with the Lord;

> Then up with yonder sacred throng,
>   We at His feet shall fall,
> And join the everlasting song,
>   And crown Him Lord of all.

CHAPTER XVIII.

THE CITY OF THE-LORD-IS-THERE.

It was in an hour of vision, when I found myself walking up a plain road with handsome guide posts on the left. Next to the index fingers on these guide posts could be seen four words welded into one—The-Lord-is-There. I felt weary with loneliness, but happy with hope. The Lord is everywhere indeed, I said, but in many places He will not allow Himself to appear, and it is the same as if He were not there. But in some places He dwells and appears. If His light can glow in a heart, and the bells of music can celebrate His presence there, why may He not dwell in a city?

In a few minutes I came to the suburbs of the city. I found that entrance was free, but that many chose to dwell on a lower plane, just outside the gate. Those within were much happier than those without, but those in the suburbs fared better than the settlers whom I had seen on the lonely roadside far away.

At the entrance of one of the gates I saw an inhabitant of the place. His countenance was exceedingly pure, and the light of joy was in his eye. "Am I in heaven, or upon the earth?"

The Hereafter. 93

I said. "You are on earth," said the man, "but strangers coming here frequently think they are in heaven, because we borrow our customs and fashions from heaven, and abide by the same laws. Indeed the place on which this city is built was selected in view of the climate, and it is a climate similar to that of heaven. People are daily traveling from here to heaven, and I am told that they encounter none of the inconvenience which comes to those who change climates." "I have read of heaven," I said, "in the book of Revelation, and your city meets the description." "And well it does," said the man, "for so it should. I will show you wherein they are alike, and wherein they differ. Do you see these walls? They are for protection and beauty; but in heaven they are for beauty only for a great gulf of space separates heaven from the wicked, and there is no danger there. Again, you see our gates open and close; but the gates of the New Jerusalem have no shutters, because there is no one near to invade. As you came up the road you met a few people who had down-cast eyes and blushing cheeks. They were leaving this city, and you would have embarrassed them greatly, if you had asked them why, for they had no reason; but in heaven there is no going out—there is no curse at the threshold."

Upon entering this city I found that it guarded the harbor on a beautiful sea, where many full rigged ships lay at anchor, and I was told that the winds which blew heavenward were more reliable than the trade winds of the East. At all hours of the day could be seen the beautiful ceremonies of an anchor-lifting, and I learned that from this port alone people could get transportation to the heavenly country.

At the close of the vision I thought of its moral:

1. There is a spiritual Zion, into which we enter at conversion. There we meet the Lord, become subjects of His kingdom and receive His sanctifying grace.

2. There is a road leading all of us to this city of Salvation, and truth and common sense teach us that the Lord is there.

3. The inhabitants of spiritual Zion observe God's laws, and seek to do His will "on earth as it is done in heaven."

4. We have possession of the only harbor from which ships sail heavenward. Ships from all other ports launch out upon a stormy sea forever.

5. The backslider has cause to blush, and no reason to allege for turning away from the Lord.

6. There is a low plane upon which moralists and unconverted church members live which may be better than to be far out in the darkness of sin, but they are not in the city of The-Lord-Is-There. Those who live in this spiritual city can say:

"Content while beholding His face,
  My all to His pleasure resigned;
No changes of season or place,
  Can make any change in my mind.
While blest with a sense of His love,
  A palace a toy would appear,
And prisons would palaces prove,
  If Jesus would dwell with me there."

CPSIA information can be obtained at www.ICGtesting.com
230785LV00001B/239/A